A DIFFERENT KIND OF DRAGON

By Derek Nelson

Illustrations by Chelsea Oram

A Kindness Crowd Book
Published by The Kindness Crowd, LLC
Copyright © 2019 by The Kindness Crowd, LLC

eBook ISBN: 978-1-7331675-1-2
Paperback ISBN: 978-1-7331675-0-5
Hardback ISBN: 978-1-7331675-2-9

For Hayden, Braxton, and all those with hemophilia
who might feel just a little bit different...

Drax was a handsome young dragon. He had green, scaly skin, sharp teeth, and powerful wings. In a few years, he would take his place among the adults of the Dragon Clan. But no matter his good looks, Drax did not feel like a dragon. You see, Drax had a BIG problem. Drax could NOT breathe fire.

All the other dragons could breathe fire. Sure, some were better than others, especially Blaster. He could hit a tree from a hundred yards away, instantly turning it to ashes. Breathing fire was what made a dragon a dragon.

Every year, the dragons held a special Fire Festival to show off their fire-breathing skills. It was always a grand celebration, with smoke rising from the forest trees for days afterward. But it was always the WORST day of the year for Drax. He had NEVER been able to breathe fire. Last year, he tried really hard, but nothing came out—at least no fire—just an awkward squawk that had Blaster laughing at him.

N ow, it was time once again for the Fire Festival, and Drax was scared. His knees shook as the others showed their talents. He wanted to hide, but he knew that sooner or later he would be called by the Dragon King to show what he could do.

Finally, it was Drax's turn. All the dragons watched to see how the one fireless dragon would perform this year.

Drax focused. "Please," he thought to himself, "just one little flame. Just enough to show them how hard I've been trying."

Drax closed his eyes for what seemed like the millionth time. He thought of his lessons, and he imagined a furnace way down deep in his belly. He felt the warm feeling rise as he took in a gigantic breath. He felt the fire building in his throat and hoped it would work this time. He let out his scream!

B ut again, no fire. Instead, a puff of steam jetted gently from his nose.

"I told you he couldn't do it!" Blaster shouted, falling to the ground with laughter. Other dragons joined in. Drax looked at their faces. He hated being laughed at. Young Drax's eyes filled with tears.

"Are we sure he's even a dragon?" Blaster said.

Drax had reached his limit. Maybe Blaster was right. Maybe he wasn't even a dragon. He didn't feel like he belonged here. He put his head down, turned, and flew away.

Drax was good at flying. He flew and he flew until his wings became sore. He didn't care where he went. He just wanted to go as far from the other dragons as possible, and he never wanted to go back.

After sunset, when his wings could take no more, Drax collapsed on the forest floor. He felt so exhausted he could barely breathe. He let his eyes close and quickly fell asleep.

Drax woke to the sun shining on his face. He thought about yesterday's Fire Festival, remembering the sick feeling in his belly. He felt lonely, but it wasn't worth returning and being known as the only non-fire-breathing dragon who had ever existed. He wondered what life would be like without the Dragon Clan.

Drax decided to fly across the kingdom. He needed to find a new place to live. He remembered hearing rumors of a human settlement far to the west. Maybe they would accept him.

As he flew west, Drax heard a sound. An unmistakable sound. It was the distress call of a fellow dragon. At first, he couldn't believe his ears. He couldn't tell where it had come from, so he changed course and let his ears lead him.

The sound led Drax to the entrance of a small cave. Looking inside, he spotted something very strange. Another dragon! It was Daphne, a youngling from the Dragon Clan. She was crying, and it made Drax's heart hurt. She rested at the back of the cave, surrounded by shiny, red rocks which cast a faint, red glow around the chamber.

Drax moved toward her. "Daphne," he whispered. "Are you okay?"

"Don't come any closer. It's a force field," Daphne said with sadness in her voice.

"Who did this?" he asked, not believing that any dragon could ever be imprisoned. Dragons were too strong. Who could possibly have captured a dragon?

"The Stone Giants," Daphne said. "As the Fire Festival ended, they came out of nowhere and started throwing boulders. Before we could fight back, several dragons had chains thrown around their necks. The Dragon Clan was in total chaos. Suddenly, a wizard with a magic staff appeared and placed a huge force field over the entire Fire Festival grounds. All the dragons are prisoners now."

"Couldn't they get away?" Drax asked.

Daphne lowered her eyes and stared at the cavern floor. "Their bodies were made of stone, and our fire was useless, Drax. No one knew what to do."

"But how did you get here?"

"I was the only one to escape at first, and they must have followed me somehow. I found this cave to rest in, but the wizard caught me. He put up the force field and said he'd be back. I'm so scared, Drax."

Drax clenched his teeth and balled his claws into fists. What could he do? Not even the fire-breathers could stop this. As his anger grew, he felt a hot, burning sensation growing strong in his belly. He could feel the fire!

He turned his head toward the wall of the cave and let out a scream. Not just any scream, but a loud, dragon scream that came from the depths of his body. As the scream burst outward, an amazing thing happened.

There was a ferocious zap as electric blue light shot out Drax's mouth. It hit the wall of the cave and blasted a big hole straight through the stone. Daphne stared at him, her mouth wide open.

"Drax! You just breathed…LIGHTNING!" she exclaimed. "No dragon has ever done that before!"

Drax tasted the electricity in his mouth. It tasted good. And for the first time ever, he felt powerful.

"Can you do it again?" Daphne asked.

"I think so," Drax said. "Stay still."

Drax focused on his breathing. He closed his eyes and took in a big breath. He imagined the lightning deep in his belly. Then he opened his mouth with a roar. Again, blue lightning flashed from his mouth, demolishing the cavern wall. The force field fell. Daphne hurried out, and they met in the forest.

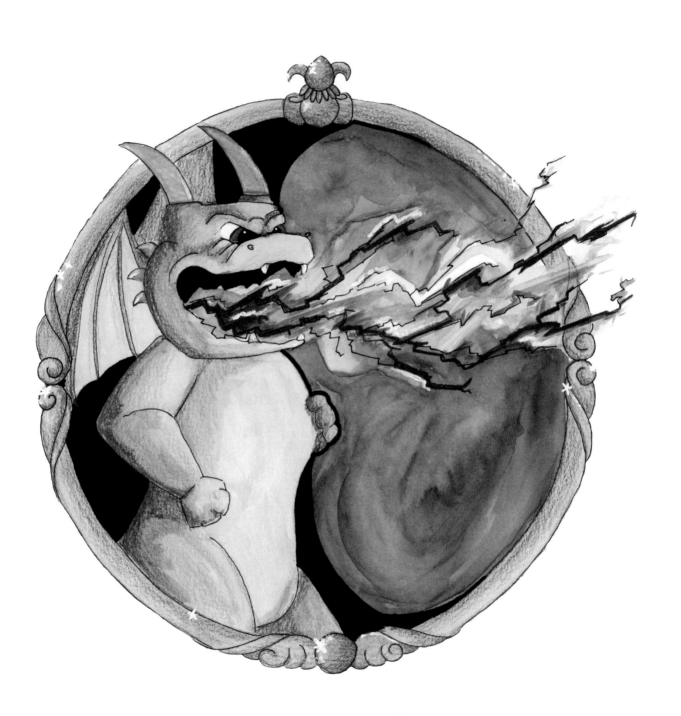

"Thank you!" she squealed. "That was amazing! How did you DO that?"

"I don't really know," Drax confessed. "I did everything they taught us about how to breathe fire, but instead, lightning came out."

"We have to help the others," Daphne said. "They need you, Drax."

The Dragon Clan had never needed him before. He wanted to help, but he felt scared.

"What about the giants?" Drax asked.

"Did you see what you did to the cave?" she reminded him. And she was right. Maybe he could help. He decided to be strong.

"Okay," Drax said. "I'm scared, but let's go back."

They didn't have far to fly. Soon they reached the edge of the Fire Festival grounds and hid behind a rock. They peeked around the edge of the rock and saw the dragons being held hostage behind a force field. Outside the force field, three solid Stone Giants stood guard.

"Maybe you can blast them," Daphne whispered. "Will you give it a try?"

"But where is the wizard?" Drax asked. He might be able to blast the Stone Giants, but he had no idea how he would attack a wizard.

"He could be anywhere," Daphne said. Drax's heart beat loud and fast in his chest.

"Stay here," Drax told Daphne. "If I can't free the dragons, I don't want the giants to know you've escaped."

"All right," she said, "and good luck." She nuzzled against him, and then Drax left.

He flew low, trying not to be seen, and set his sights on the giants.

As he neared them, he focused on his belly and felt the lightning begin to build. He couldn't wait to blast them!

The Stone Giants had no time to react. Drax was upon them in an instant.

A powerful streak of blue light shot from his mouth. It hit one of the Stone Giants square in the chest!

... AND NOTHING HAPPENED.

Drax had expected the Stone Giant to shatter, to be blasted to bits. His eyes grew wide, and he held his breath. He didn't know what to do.

And then, next to the giants, a large puff of smoke appeared. In the middle of the smoke stood the wizard. Drax's heart sank.

The wizard wore long, purple robes. His hair flowed in silver waves around his shoulders, and his hands gripped a menacing magic staff. He lifted the staff skyward, then crashed it down into the earth.

Drax stopped flying in midair. His wings stopped working. He expected to fall to the ground, but somehow, he stayed suspended, unable to move. The wizard had him under a spell.

"You should never have come back here, dragon!" the wizard's voice boomed. "Now, you will join the others!"

The wizard scowled, and a fireball formed at the tip of his staff. He was going to throw it at Drax!

While the wizard focused on him, Drax noticed Daphne in the distance. She flew toward the wizard REALLY fast. Just as he started to throw the fireball, she hit the wizard from behind. The fireball exploded upon impact, and she fell to the earth, unmoving.

The impact threw the wizard across the ground, and the staff lay just out of his reach.

Daphne's collision broke the spell over Drax, who now flew fast toward the wizard. Drax aimed at the staff, and he let out a roar!

Blue lightning rocketed from Drax's mouth and hit the staff perfectly. A tremendous explosion shook the skies, and the staff shattered into tiny pieces.

The force field imprisoning the Dragon Clan disappeared, and immediately the sky filled with dragons. They were free! They attacked the Stone Giants and pounded them with their mighty tails.

The wizard slowly lifted his head and looked at the pieces of his staff scattered all around. He'd been beaten. He struggled to his feet, and with a whirlwind wave of his hand, the wizard disappeared in a cloud of smoke. Without the wizard, the Stone Giants turned and ran for the hills.

Drax turned his attention to Daphne. She had saved him when his plan went wrong. His heart swelled with gratitude. Drax rested his head against hers, letting his tears fall freely.

The Dragon Clan gathered around Daphne's motionless body. As Drax wept, Daphne slowly opened her eyes. "What happened, Drax?" she whispered.

"It's okay. The dragons are free," Drax said. "You saved us."

"Let's give her time to rest," said the Dragon King, and the dragons moved Daphne to a soft spot of earth.

That evening, when Daphne had recovered, the dragons gathered at the festival grounds. Drax took in a long, slow breath and admired the beautiful sunset.

Blaster approached Drax and touched him lightly on the shoulder.

"Thank you, Drax," he said. "I'm sorry I made fun of you at the Fire Festival. Without you, we would still be slaves to the giants."

"I appreciate your apology," Drax said, "and I forgive you."

Blaster nodded, then left to join the other younglings.

The last rays of sunlight began to fade.

"That was very brave, you two," said the Dragon King to Drax and Daphne. "I don't know what we would have done without you. We will never forget your courage. And Drax, be careful with that breath of yours. We may have to start a Lightning Festival soon."

Drax looked around and smiled, for he finally felt like a dragon.

THE END

Acknowledgements

The greatest joy of my life is being connected to amazing human beings. A big thank you to all who made this book possible. It would never have happened without the support of so many people. Whether you helped shape the story, edit the manuscript, or simply encouraged me to keep going, I truly appreciate the help you provided along the journey. Special thanks to Krisdee Nelson, Hayden Morgan, Braxton Nelson, Bella Nelson, Karlee Nelson, Chelsea Oram, Jimmy Redquest, Richard Mupfudze, Eddie and Kimmie Scott, Chris and Jess Bombardier, Suha Patel, Erik Melde, Kelly Ryan, Daniel Lancaster, Tiffanee Worley, Jay R. Morgan, Maria Perez, Ally Remigio, Laurie Kelley, Rosa Sophia, Jed Jurchenko, Hynek Palatin, and all my hemophilia family around the world.

To access additional resources related to this book, please visit

www.TheKindnessCrowd.com

Made in the USA
Coppell, TX
20 March 2020